The Big Match

John Goodwin

NEWCASTLE-UNDER-LYME
COLLEGE LIBRARY

Published in association with
The Basic Skills Agency

Acknowledgements
Cover: Shane Marsh
Illustrations: Jim Eldridge

Orders; please contact Bookpoint Ltd, 39 Milton Park, Abingdon, Oxon OX14
4TD. Telephone: (44) 01235 400414, Fax: (44) 01235 400454. Lines are open
from 9.00–6.00, Monday to Saturday, with a 24 hour message answering service.
Email address: orders@bookpoint.co.uk

British Library Cataloguing in Publication Data
A catalogue record for this title is available from the British Library

ISBN 0 340 77469 X

First published 2000
Impression number 10 9 8 7 6 5 4 3 2 1
Year   2005 2004 2003 2002 2001 2000

Typeset by GreenGate Publishing Services, Tonbridge, Kent.
Printed in Great Britain for Hodder and Stoughton Educational, a division of
Hodder Headline Plc, 338 Euston Road, London NW1 3BH, by Atheneum
Press, Gateshead, Tyne & Wear

The Big Match

Contents

1

Red Card Dad

I don't mind a game of football.
Sometimes it can be a real laugh.
But there's one thing I hate.
I hate having to play football with my dad.
A few weeks ago he put on his shorts and said,
'Game of footie, Danny?'
I kept my head down like I hadn't heard him.
Some hope.
'It's time for a bit of fun,' he said.

I knew all about his 'bit of fun'.
I broke my leg and he had his arm in a sling
for weeks last time we had a bit of fun.
The trouble is my dad is like a little kid.
He's never grown up.

'Footie – out in the garden,' he said.
'No Dad. Not the garden.'
'Come on.'
I knew we were in for trouble.
Our garden is no bigger than a postage stamp.

'Bit of tackling.'
'No Dad. You'll ...'
It was too late. Crunch went his foot.
Splat went my mum's best roses.
Smack went the ball.
Snap went her snap dragons.
I picked up the ball.
'Foul!' screamed Dad.
'You're the dirty fouler Dad.
Look at the state of this garden,' I said.

Next we had to do penalties.
He was marking out the goal
before I could stop him.
'Below the drainpipe and between the doors,'
he said.
'No Dad.'
'You get in goal and I'll shoot.'
'No way.'

He wouldn't take no for an answer.
So I stood under the drainpipe
and in between the doors.

He was already placing the ball on the ground.
I knew he was going to blast it.
Blast it hard.
I looked up at the drainpipe.
I hoped it wouldn't come crashing down on my
head if he hit the ball too high.
I wanted to run out of the way.
But it was too late.
Dad's stupid banana legs had started to move.
Faster and faster they hurtled.
Blast off was only seconds away.

Then my mother arrived.
She drove along the road hooting her car horn
louder than any ref's whistle.
My dad's feet slid to a stop.
Perhaps he thought
he was going to get the red card.
He picked up the football
and drove off in his old van.
I didn't see him for weeks.
Dad doesn't live with us any more.
When he does visit us it always means trouble.

2

Dads v Kids

The parcel arrived early one morning.
'It's from your dad,' said Mum.
'A parcel for me? But it's not my birthday.'
I opened up the parcel.
Inside was a football shirt.
Not England or Man U or even
Newcastle kit.
It was a pale green shirt with
        DADS v KIDS
printed on it in big black writing.
I was gob smacked.

'Did Dad say anything?'

'No.'

'But why did he bring me this?'

That question troubled me all day.
Dad did strange things sometimes.
This was going to be one of those times.
I knew it for sure.

When I got home from school
there he was in our kitchen.
He was wearing a football shirt.
It was just like the one in the parcel.

'What do you think, Danny?' he said.
He was showing off his shirt
like a model at a fashion show.
I didn't say anything.
'Are you up for it then?' he asked.
'Up for what?'
'For a great football match.
Dads against Kids.
You get your own team of kids.
I'll sort out a dads' team.
We'll play the match a week on Saturday. OK?'
'No Dad,' I said.
But he wasn't listening to me.
'I'll sort it all out.
You just turn up with your mates.'

Next day at dinner time at school Wozza says,
'Who's your forwards then?'
'What?'
'Are you playing a 4–4–2?'
'No. I'm eating chips.
I'm not playing anything,' I said.
'Yes you are.
You're captain of the Kids' team,' he said.
Later on Crabbie passed me a note.
'*I don't mind being a sub.*
Just put me in your squad.'
I sent him a note back
'*I can put you at right back.*
Right back off the pitch. Forget it.'

On the way back home from school
loads of kids came up to me.
They all said their dads were in the team
and could I pick them for my team?

3

Danny for Captain

'Mum do you know where Dad is?'
I said when I got home. She didn't look at me.
'He must be somewhere', I said.
'Look in the paper,' said Mum.
Had she lost it or what?
I looked in our local paper,
On the sports page it said in big letters
             COME ON YOU DADS
There was a picture of my dad too.

It also said I was pleased to be captain
of the Kids' team.
'Pleased to be!' What a load of rubbish.

Half an hour later Dad came round.
Only now he wasn't smiling
like his picture in the paper.
He looked straight at me and asked,
'So why don't you want to be captain?'
It went very quiet. I didn't know what to say.
I couldn't say, 'Because I think
you're a prat.'

His eyes met mine and he said very quietly,
'I've done it all for you.'
My anger melted away like an ice-cream melts
on a hot summer's day.
'I know I've not been the best dad,' he said.
'So I thought I'd try to make a big effort.'
Then he started to smile.
'Besides,' he said, 'Elroy Gibbs
is going to be at the match.
He'll present a cup to the winning team.
I know Elroy is your hero.'

Too right.
Elroy has been my football hero for ages.
'So do you want to shake hands with Elroy?
Yes or no?'
Of course I did.
So I decided I had to be positive.
I would be captain.
The Kids were going to win.
Nothing less than a 3–0 victory would do.
Elroy Gibbs had better look out.
He had some serious hand shaking to do.

4

Spying on the Dads

Players swarmed round the ball.
They were like bees round a honey pot.
I ran up the touch line shouting at them,
'Kick it out. Go back. Stay back.
Push up Ravi, Pass it Tommo.
PASS IT NOW!'

It was hopeless.
The more I shouted the worse they played.

The backs were forward.
The forwards were back.
Nobody but nobody passed the ball.
Both goalies were useless.
One couldn't catch a bag of chips
let alone a football.
The other kept falling asleep.
At the end of the 7-a-side match
I had a word with them all.

'This is terrible,' I said.
'We have only one practice game left
before the big match.
We'll get hammered if we play like this.
We'd be a push over for nippers in nappies.
The playgroup would thrash us.
The Dads will be tough. Big hard Dads.
We've got to get it together.'

I was walking back home. I felt bad.
Wozza came up behind me.
'It can't be that bad,' he said.
'It is.'
'You need to make some changes.
You play in goal. Put Tommo as a striker.'
'Tommo … a striker. You must be joking.'
'He can do it,' said Wozza.
'Just give him a chance.'
I began to think about what Wozza had said.
'Do you fancy spying?' I asked him.
'Spying?'

'Yes. The Dads are having a practice.
We could go down the sports centre
and see them.'

We went to the sports centre.
Sitting on the bonnet of his old van
was my dad and a few of his mates.

They weren't even kicking a ball about.
They were drinking beer out of cans
and smoking fags.
We spied on them through a gap in the fence.
'We can beat those boozers,' said Wozza.
'No sweat.'

Then the boozers saw us. They came over.
'What's this then?' said Dad.
'You spying on our game plan.'
'That was no game plan.
You were just boozing,' I said.
'We can beat you any day,' said Wozza.
'Oh yes?' said Dad.
'Oh yes?' said all his mates.
'You better look out,' said Dad,
'We've got a secret weapon.'
'Secret weapon,' repeated his mates.
The war of words was over.
It was time for the big match.
Now was the time for action.

5

The Secret
Weapon

SMACK! The secret weapon was in full power.
He was huge.
He was a massive bloke called Trev.
The ground shook under his giant boots.
The ball looked tiny at his feet. On he came.
He didn't bother to pass the ball.
He just thundered up the pitch.
Nearer. Nearer to me in goal.
All our team ran away from him.
They were in panic.

'Tackle him. Somebody tackle him,' I shouted.
But it was useless. Nobody dared go near him.
My legs were like jelly.
Only Ravi and I stood between
Big Trev and the goal.
Ravi wasn't running away.
He just stood and waited.
Closer came the secret weapon.

'Look out Ravi,' shouted Wozza.
'He'll knock you flat,' screamed Crabbie.
'Run for your life,' shouted Tommo.
But still Ravi didn't move.
Big Trev saw him now and began to laugh.
Louder and louder he laughed.
Still Ravi didn't move.
He had his eyes on the ball
at the giant's feet.
Then the ball hit a lump in the pitch.
It bobbled off to the right.
Quick as a flash Ravi made a move.
He darted forward.

With both feet sliding he went for the ball.
His feet skidded into the ball.
It was knocked away towards the touchline.
Soon it would be out of play.
Then we could regroup.

But Big Trev was too good.
He lifted up his huge foot.
He made a high leap in the air
right over Ravi's feet.
In the same move he knocked the ball
back from the touchline.
Then he had the ball at his feet again.
He sprinted towards the goal.
I could see him coming closer and closer.

ZAP! went his foot. WHACK! went the ball.
I didn't even see it coming.
The cannon ball was right on target.
It smashed into the back of the net.
We had played three minutes of football
and we were 1–0 down.

Dad was shouting 'yeeees!' as I bent down
to pick up the ball from the back of the net.

'One nil … one nil,'
chanted the rest of the Dads.

At that moment a big silver car
drove into the ground.
Was this Elroy Gibbs coming to see me
make a real fool of myself?
I looked hard at the car.
I tried to make out who was the driver.

'Come on. Get on with the game,'
shouted one of the Dads.
I tried to forget about the car.
Perhaps it was best
not to see who the driver was.

'Come on. Keep it tight,' I shouted.
I tried to sound cool. But I felt terrible.
Ravi had been the only player
to go near the ball. Things looked grim.

Things soon went from bad to worse.
A few minutes later we were 2–0 down.
The secret weapon ran all the way with the ball.
Then he cracked it in the back of the net.
I once saw a team lose 27–0.
It was no match and no fun.
Perhaps we were going to lose 27–0, too.

Soon Big Trev was running down the
pitch again.
I knew I had to do something. But what?
My feet started to move.
It was like they had a will of their own.
Out of the goal I ran.

'Danny! Danny get back,' shouted Wozza.

But it was too late. On I ran.

If nobody would tackle Big Trev then I would.

Further and further out of goal I ran.

'Get back,' shouted Wozza again.

The giant saw me coming.

He laughed one of his loud laughs.

I didn't care. It was tackle or bust.

We were running straight at each other.

I wasn't going to stop. Oh no. Not me.

NOW! said a voice in my head.
I went into the tackle.
Both my feet slid on the ground.
The ball and the giant's legs were so close.
But Big Trev was too smart for me.
He side-stepped very fast. I'd gone too soon.
My tackle had failed. I fell flat.

I'd left an open goal. Big Trev looked
to the goal. It seemed so easy.
With one kick he would score his hat trick.
Nothing could stop him.

WHACK! went his foot.
It was so fast. Too fast.
His foot didn't hit the ball.
It crunched into the ground
in front of the ball.
Then his leg buckled under him.
With a cry of pain he crashed to the ground.

6

In With a Chance

We had to stop the game.
The Dads carried off their secret weapon.
He had to lie down in the changing rooms.
'We're down to ten,' said Dad.
'We've got no subs.'
It was time for a tactic talk.
'Look, it's hard luck for them.
But our good luck.
Without Big Trev they're lost.
We can win this yet.
We need a quick goal,' I said.

But no quick goal came.
The whistle went for half-time
and we were still 2–0 down.
My mum came onto the pitch.
'How are your legs?' she said to Dad.
'Bad,' he said. 'But I'll survive.'
Dad had a disease when he was a kid.
That's why his legs are like bananas.

I looked at Dad again.
He'd really wanted to play this match.
But why? What was he hoping to prove?
I was going over to talk to him.
But the whistle went for the second half.

Time was running out.
There were only fifteen minutes of the
match left.
We were still 2–0 down.
But the Dads were tired.
Too many beers and fags
were slowing them down.

Dad played as striker.
He tried to keep his legs pumping
up and down the pitch.
But by now he was walking and not running.
A long ball was kicked up to him.
With a swing of his foot he kicked the ball
clean out of the ground.
All the Dads lay on the ground
like a pile of empty beer cans.
It took ages to get the ball back.

When we did get the ball back
Ravi took a quick throw in.
Half the Dads were still lazing about.
'Wait,' shouted one.
'Hang about,' said another.
But it was too late.
Ravi threw to Tommo. Tommo passed to Wozza.
Wozza passed to Crabbie.
Crabbie went flying down the centre.
He was soon in their penalty area.
He looked up for a second
and let fly a slow hard shot.

The Dads' goalie stopped the ball.
It bounced out of his hands
into the corner of the net.
'Goooal,' shouted Wozza. 'What a striker!'

It was a turning point.
At last we began to play as a team.
We put neat passes together.
We pressed hard for that second goal.
'Back,' shouted Dad. 'Back in defence.'
All the Dads fell back.
They crowded the goal mouth.
It was a big mistake.
Ten minutes is a short time.
But in football it can seem a lifetime.

We won a corner.
The ball came over high in the air.
Crabbie jumped high above the wall
of tired Dads.
He headed the ball cleanly into the goal.
It was 2–2.

Before we had chance to score the winner
the ref blew his whistle.
It was the end of the match.

A car door opened.
Onto the pitch walked Elroy Gibbs.
'Great match. Great comeback, Kids,' he said.
'What about a penalty shootout.
Then you can have a winner.'
'Yea,' shouted the Kids.
I looked at Dad. His face was very red.
His legs seemed more like bananas than ever.
Yet he was smiling.
Smiling like I hadn't seen him do before.
'Let's keep it as a draw,' I said.

I've still got the football shirt
of that big match.
I've grown too big for it now.
We still don't see much of Dad.
But I'll always keep the shirt.
It reminds me of a time
when I almost understood him.